A Spider Named Apollo

Adventures of a Multi-legged Music Lover

Written by Jeanne Merkle Sorrell and Jeannette Sorrell

Illustrated by Gail M. Nelson

A Spider Named Apollo is written by Jeanne Merkle Sorrell and Jeannette Sorrell, and illustrated by Gail M. Nelson.

Layout and Cover Design by e-book-design.com

ISBN 978-0-692-79959-8

Printed in the United States of America.

Dedications

Released in honor of the 25th Anniversary Season of Apollo's Fire, this book of Apollo's musical adventures is dedicated to the young and young-at-heart who have discovered their love of music at Apollo's Fire concerts. The passionate support of the audience and patrons in these 25 years has nurtured this special orchestra – allowing a generation of young people to grow up with the joy and emotion that rings through baroque music.

—Jeanne and Jeannette Sorrell

I would like to dedicate this book to my daughter, Katie, whose love for music is a wonderful inspiration.

—Gail Nelson

Listen to the Music!

To hear Apollo's Fire play Mozart's *The Magic Flute* just like Apollo the Spider did, please visit:

www.apollosfire.org/apollo/magicflute.html/

Have you ever squished a spider? Many people do. But some spiders are nice, like me.

We eat nasty pests in your home that could be harmful. And we have interesting lives...

I'm a Cellar Spider. (Don't confuse me with a Daddy long legs!) I grew up in a dark corner of a church in Cleveland, Ohio. When my 26 brothers and sisters and I came out of Mama's egg sac, everyone was pointing and looking at me strangely. They all had eight legs. For some reason, I had ten.

Everyone laughed because I was different. I felt shy and lonely and confused.

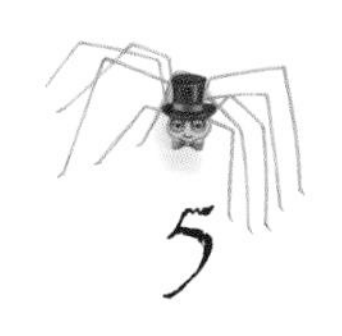

One day I was wandering through the church alone and I heard beautiful music. I followed the sound down the hall, up the stairs, around the corner, and came upon... an orchestra! There were 15 musicians playing beautiful music together. I saw a program lying on the pew and it said "Apollo's Fire Baroque Orchestra."

I loved the name!

At that moment I decided to call myself Apollo.

I spied a microphone hanging from the ceiling. So I crawled up high to listen. "Hanging out" at the rehearsals, I felt so happy. If you look carefully, you can see me!

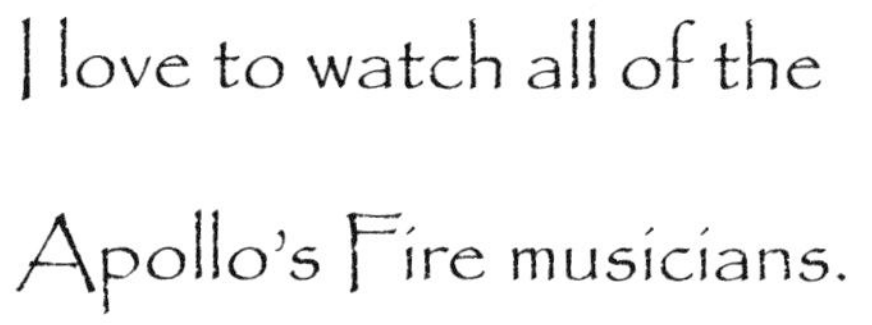

I love to watch all of the Apollo's Fire musicians.

The *viola da gamba* looks like a cello but sounds softer. It has a nickname—gamba. Mr. René plays both the gamba and the cello. His fingers move so fast!

The violin players look so graceful as their bows move across the strings! When the bows move fast, the music gets very excited. If only I could play the violin!

I love to watch Miss Sue play the bass. She plucks the strings and makes a low, low sound that is beautiful. But the bass is VERY big! I don't think I could play the bass, even with ten legs.

There are lots

of wind instruments:

flutes, recorders, oboes,

horns, and trumpets.

The loudest is the trumpet.

Shhh! Please don't tell the musicians, but I do not really like the trumpet. It is VERY loud and shrill, and once almost shook me off my perch on the microphone!

I love the harpsichord best. The director, Miss Jeannette, plays the harpsichord. I love watching her fingers race up and down the keys. Sometimes I close my eyes and imagine myself playing the harpsichord. Some people say that spiders cannot play harpsichords, but I don't believe it. After all, I have as many legs as Jeannette has fingers!

I learned that Apollo's Fire is a special orchestra that plays with very old instruments. Most of the music they play is called *Baroque*.

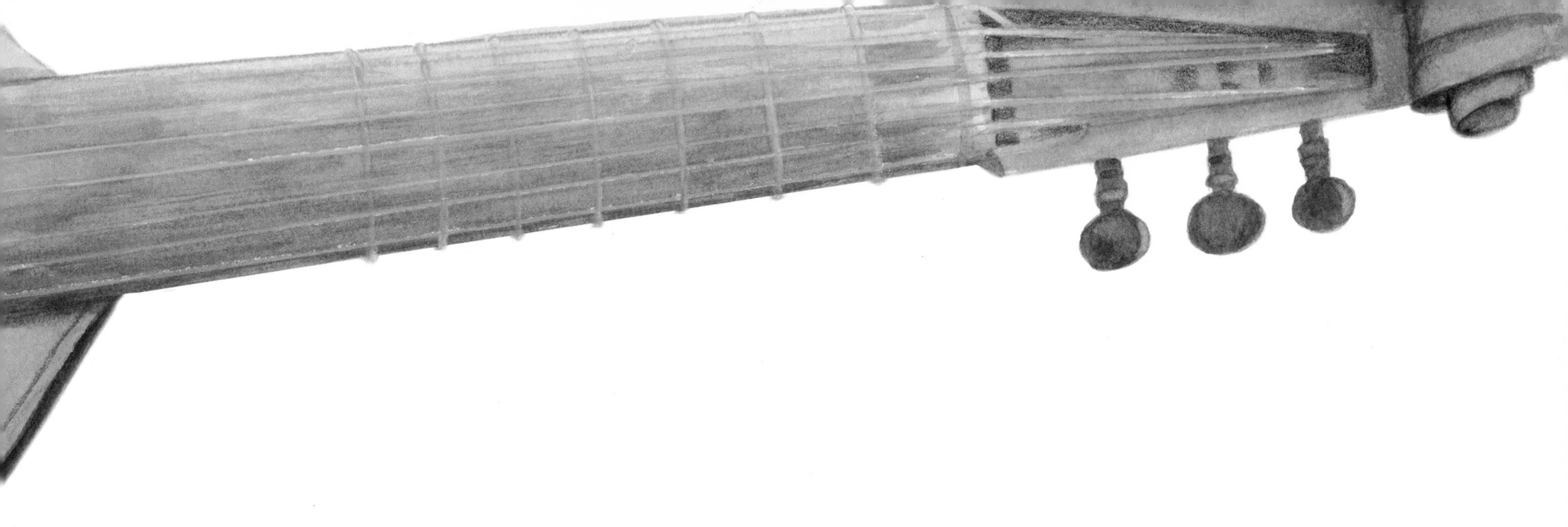

I think their music is beautiful. It helps me forget about being lonely. But I wish I had a friend to share the music with.

At least, I have learned that my ten legs are useful. They help me run very fast so that I don't get squished. And they help me dance the samba—and maybe one day, play the gamba.

One day the musicians were very excited. They were preparing for a special concert - an opera! It would be held in a beautiful place called Severance Hall. The opera was called *The Magic Flute*, by the composer Mozart. I learned that an opera is a musical story, acted out in costume. Two thousand people were expected to come to the concert!

I was determined to follow the musicians to Severance Hall
and hear this opera. But how to get there?
Then I thought of a clever plan.

When the musicians went on a coffee break from their practicing, I spun a long, long silk web and carefully crawled from my microphone perch, down, down—right into the inside of Jeannette's green harpsichord! I found a comfortable corner for hiding.

That evening, after the musicians had finished practicing, Mr. Tom, the stage manager, came and took the harpsichord away to Jeannette's house. This was my first hitch-hiking experience, riding in a harpsichord!

The next week went by so fast. I "hung out" in Miss Jeannette's harpsichord at her house as she practiced many hours. It was fun to be inside the harpsichord and feel the music vibrating!

But then something happened that I did not expect.
The day before the concert, Mr. Tom came to
Miss Jeannette's house with a strange instrument.
I heard Jeannette call it a *glockenspiel.*
Mr. Tom called it a *Glock.* I love the name: "Glock."

But suddenly I panicked! Miss Jeannette was not going to play the harpsichord for the concert at beautiful Severance Hall. She was going to play the Glock! I needed to act fast. So that night, when Jeannette was sleeping, I crawled out of the harpsichord and climbed into the Glock. Once inside, I felt quite cozy.

Finally, the concert-day arrived. I was so excited! I dressed up in my very best hat and bow-tie. Mr. Tom wrapped the Glock in its soft brown cover, placed it carefully in a van, and drove down the hill to Severance Hall. Then he placed it on the stage.

When I finally dared to peek out over the top of the Glock, I could hardly believe my eyes.

There was a beautiful painted ceiling and a huge stage surrounded by gold organ pipes. Around the edges of the theatre were special box seats. It was the most beautiful place I had ever seen!

I wondered where to hang so that I could see the concert.

I spied the perfect place—Box 2—which was high up,

right across from the stage.

I spun a silk web from the orchestra seats on the bottom

floor, up to Box 2, and simply climbed up!

I attached myself to the railing

and waited...

I looked down and saw people arriving far below me. There were people of all ages—some who looked very old and also quite a few children. Most of them were dressed elegantly. I was so glad that I had worn my top hat and bow tie. Phew!

The orchestra and chorus walked on stage and sat down. I could feel the excitement. Then the audience applauded as the first violinist walked out on stage. He is called the concertmaster. He looked so elegant! He played a note on the Glock, and all of the strings played the same note to check their tuning.

Finally, Miss Jeannette walked out on the stage.

We all clapped. She looked very happy.

She stood at the conductor's podium

and raised her arms, holding a baton

in her right hand. Then she lowered

her arms and the music began—

the Overture!

I knew, from listening to rehearsals of Apollo's Fire, that the Overture is the orchestra piece at the beginning of an opera, before the story begins.

The whole orchestra played some majestic chords, full of suspense. The music rose to my perch on the railing. Jeannette pointed at the second violins and they suddenly began to play a fast and bouncy theme. I was impressed that all seven violins could be so together!

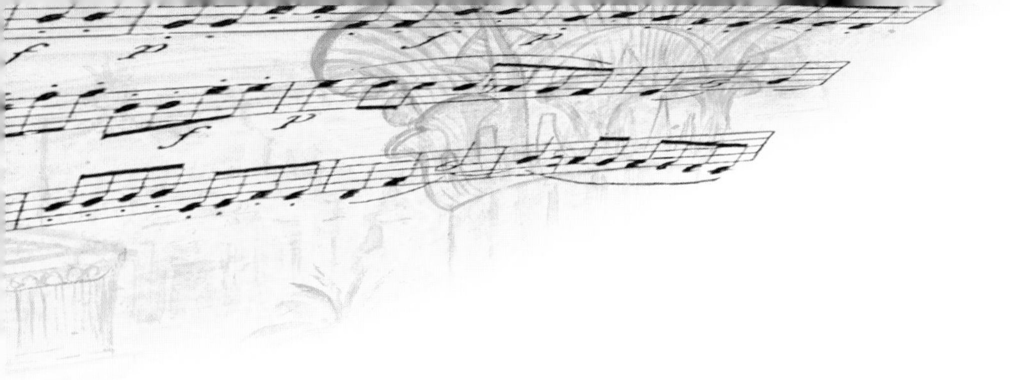

Then Jeannette pointed at other sections of the orchestra, one after the other, and soon everyone was playing this fast and bouncy theme, at different times! But very coordinated. It sounded amazing! It was the most beautiful music I had ever heard. I fell in love with Mozart.

The Overture came to an end with fantastic chords from the whole orchestra, and big drums called the timpani. It was THRILLING!
The audience applauded wildly, and I
applauded with all my available legs.

Miss Jeannette cued the orchestra again and they began some dark and stormy music. The lights lowered. The story was beginning.

And then I had a BIG surprise.

A large DRAGON came out! And the dragon had ten legs, just like me! He was a cute dragon, not very scary, really. The Dragon was chasing a prince named Tamino. They ran around the orchestra, back and forth, as Tamino tried bravely to battle the Dragon. It looked pretty funny!

Then suddenly three beautiful Ladies arrived. One of them grabbed Miss Jeannette's conducting baton out of her hand! And she used it to stab the Dragon.

The Dragon fell "dead" on the stage, rolled on his back and wiggled his ten legs in the air. Everyone giggled.

Then I realized that
this "Dragon" was
made of five people—
dancers who all
moved
together.

Amazing!

The first part of the concert seemed to go by very fast.

There was a character named Papageno
who had a colorful costume of feathers
and played some magic bells.
He was very funny, but also
a bit sad. And there was
Prince Tamino who
had a beautiful
Magic Flute.

Then it was time for intermission. And a scary thing happened. I looked up from the railing and saw a lady in the front of the box pointing at me. She gave her handkerchief to the man next to her and kept pointing at me. I suddenly realized with horror that she wanted the man to squish me! I saw my life flash before my eyes!

With the speed of light, I scurried into a small hole in the railing and hid. I was really *appalled* that even people at a Mozart concert would want to squish a spider. Shocking!

Finally, the musicians came back and the music began again. I carefully crawled out of my hiding place to watch. The coast was clear—the nasty couple were completely absorbed in the music.

Papageno sang a sad song about wanting to find a girlfriend just like him, with feathers. I brushed away tears, as I too wanted to find someone who loved music, like me, and would be my friend.

But the opera had a happy ending! An ugly old hag was magically changed into a beautiful young girl—Papagena!

Papageno and Papagena sang a joyous duet together and ran off as the audience applauded wildly. I saw some people brush happy tears from their eyes. I did too, thinking how nice it would be to have a friend like Papagena.

Miss Jeannette and the musicians bowed and bowed. They walked off stage and on stage, off stage and on stage, as the audience stood up and kept clapping. I clapped hard too.

I got so excited that I clapped all ten legs at once and fell off my perch,

down,

down,

to the

floor

below.

I landed on a soft, blue velvet seat. Luckily it was empty so that I didn't alarm any ladies! The concert was over. I brushed myself off and watched the musicians leave the stage. They looked so happy!

"Hello there," cheeped a small, high voice below me.

I looked around but saw no one.

"Where are you?" I asked.

"I'm down here, under the seat," cheeped the small voice.

I quickly hopped down to the floor, and soon found myself face to face with... a Cricket.

"Hi, I'm Apollo," I said. "Who are you?"

"I'm Apollina," said the Cricket. "We have almost the same names!"

"What are you doing here?" I asked.

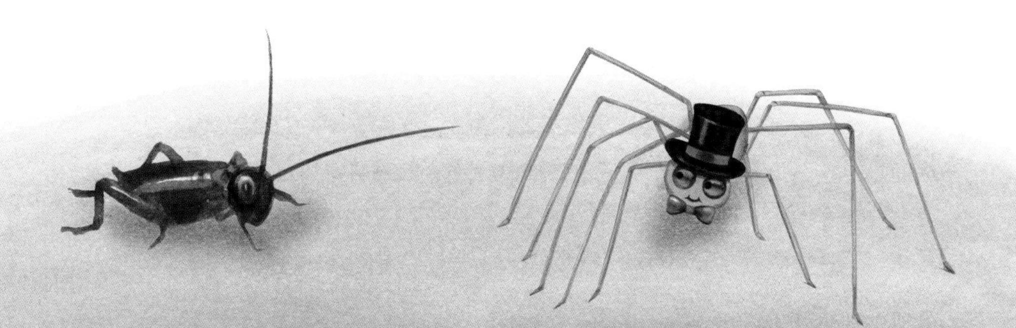

"I really love music," said Apollina. "When I get lonely, I make chirping music by rubbing my wings together. But I especially love Mozart's music. I like his piano concertos best, but *The Magic Flute* is pretty great, too. By the way, which do you prefer, the violin or the gamba?"

"I don't know. I love them both," I answered, feeling embarrassed. Apollina knew so much about music! "What I DO know," I said, "is... I sure would love to play the Glock with you."

The concert hall was now empty. Only the Glock was left on the stage.

"Come on!" said Apollina. "Spin a web up to the stage and take me with you! Show me that Glock before Mr. Tom takes it away."

And off we went—

me and my new friend.

About the Authors

Jeanne Sorrell, Ph. D., has spent most of her career as a professor of nursing and research. The author of over 125 articles in scholarly journals, she also enjoys creative writing. She collaborated with her nursing students in writing a children's book, *The Magic Stethoscope*, to encourage young people to consider a career in nursing. She is also the author of an award-winning play, *Six Characters in Search of an Answer*, based on interviews conducted with persons with Alzheimer's and their caregivers. She hopes that children who read *A Spider Named Apollo* will come to love baroque music as much as Apollo does.

Jeannette Sorrell, *conductor and harpsichordist*, is honored to collaborate with her mother in writing this book. As a child, she was a bit shy and lonely like Apollo, and took up the violin at age 9. She was thrilled by orchestra concerts and loved playing the violin in the school orchestra. At the age of 10, she spent a year practicing the piano on a paper keyboard until her family acquired a piano. She has gone on to perform as conductor and harpsichordist on some of the world's most renowned stages, including the BBC Proms in London, the Royal Theatre of Madrid, the Tanglewood Festival, and the Aspen Music Festival.

About the Illustrator

Gail M. Nelson is passionate about books in all forms. She loves to draw, paint, and help authors bring their books to life. Her favorite expression is, "Books are chocolate for my soul."

Gail graduated with a Master's degree in fine art and she has been a freelance artist, illustrator, and graphic designer since 1984. She makes her home in the mountains of Colorado with her husband, dog, and the wild turkeys, deer, chipmunks, rabbits, hummingbirds... and spiders!